Anthony Matre

The Living Statue

A Comedy in four Acts

Anthony Matre

The Living Statue
A Comedy in four Acts

ISBN/EAN: 9783337252939

Printed in Europe, USA, Canada, Australia, Japan

Cover: Foto ©Andreas Hilbeck / pixelio.de

More available books at **www.hansebooks.com**

....The ....

Living * Statue,

A COMEDY IN FOUR ACTS,

Adapted from the German.

...BY...

ANTHONY MATRE,

Teacher of St. Philomena's School, ...CINCINNATI, O.

...AUTHOR OF...

"St. Lawrence,"   "Tarcisius,"   "St. Philomena,"
"Rome under Valerian,"   "The Grecian Princess,"
"Fabiola," Etc.

CINCINNATI, O.
Jos. Berning Printing Co., 431 Main Street.
1898.

Cast of Characters.

PLETZER, German Burgomaster of Dingsda.

ALOYS, his son.

O'KEEFE, Irish Police Officer.

SEVENSHOE, A Fake Artist.

SCHMITT, a Cook, formerly in Pletzer's employ.

FIRST COUNCILMAN,

SECOND COUNCILMAN,

THIRD COUNCILMAN,

FOURTH COUNCILMAN,

} of Dingsda.

COURIER, from the Chief of Police.

STEIGER, a Farmer.

Police, Farmers, Populace.

ACT I.

AN APARTMENT IN PLETZER'S HOUSE.

PLETZER. (*Reads; stops suddenly.*) Pshaw, these stringent times will soon cause my death. A fortnight has elapsed since my fellow-citizens have elected me burgomaster of this thriving little city Dingsda, and I feel very proud of the distinction. Since I am in office I have been thinking of a plan how I could undertake something which would benefit my sixhundred Dingsda friends, and which would make me renowned in all the world.—Just as Macedonia was too small for Alexander the Great, so is Dingsda too small for all my plans.—Columbus and I, Dingsda and America!—More I need not say. But in spite of this ungrateful world, I will try to become the Columbus of Dingsda and immortalize my name.

But how? That's the serious question. (*He meditates; then takes paper and reads:*)

Krautwinkel, Feb. 25, 1853.

Fellow-citizens:

A mass-meeting will be held at the town-hall next Thursday to make plans and accept contributions for the erection of a suitable monument in honor of our distinguished fellow-companion, the world-renowned shoemaker and editor, Col. Flinzer, who for twenty long years edited the Sulsbacher Calendar, and who died recently, leaving his family in destitute circumstances. It now remains, fellow-citizens, for you to show your esteem and veneration for the works and merits of this great Krautwinkler genius. To show our gratitude, it will be advisable to erect a grand monument of sandstone in honor of the deceased, which shall serve as a mark of generosity to our present and future generation. All communications may be addressed to the office of this paper.—

(*Pletzer rises enthusiastically*)

I have it! I have it! What Krautwinkel can do, Dingsda can more than accomplish. And if the people of Krautwinkel intend to use sandstone for their statue we will erect one of granite and gain a European fame. The statue must be a life sized one and represent a person on a horse or mule. A beautiful iron fence must surround it. — — — — (*Walks up and down the stage.*)

Enter O'Keefe. (Comical Irishman.)

O'KEEFE. (*Out of breath. He tries to speak.*)

PLETZER. O'Keefe. O'Keefe, at last I have found it; I have found it!

O'KEEFE.. (*Opens his mouth, but can't utter a wora.*)

PLETZER. O'Keefe a great thought just entered my mind; we must erect a statue on the market place.

O'KEEFE. (*Joyfully.*) That is indeed — a great thought — Lord burgomaster. — Yes, we must erect a statue — in Dingsda. — That will make *our* names immortal. (*Pietzer bows.*) Our names will be recorded in history; our names will be placed in the corner stone; yes, all papers will speak and write of us. Hurrah!

PLETZER.   Yes, just think of the honor that will be in store for us! Our little town will improve; the statue will attract many strangers; Dingsda will be chosen as a convention place for artists, tourists, and professors; it will be found necessary to build a railway to our town; I will be obliged to rebuild my humble inn into a large hotel; you, O'Keefe, will be the city's professional guide and earn many an extra dollar.—

O'KEEFE.   Lord Pletzer, a great thought also entered my mind,—a thought that seconds and fully coincides with yours,—a thought which will make our town still more famous.

PLETZER.   (*Looks at him as if to ask a question.*)

O'KEEFE.   The statue must be made by a native artist; by an artist born in Dingsda.

PLETZER.   (*Looking doubtfully.*)

O'KEEFE.   But, Lord Pletzer, are you so forgetful? Don't you recollect that three years ago the young Sevenshoe was sent to Munich, at the expense of our good town, to learn sculpturing? He surely must be far advanced in the art by this time, and can easily gratify our demands.

PLETZER. Oh yes, I well remember him now. The young Sevenshoe who showed such great talent in drawing; and who went to school with my Aloys; and played so many tricks — — — (*In thoughts.*) Yes, yes, this young Sevenshoe must be recalled. It is now his turn to show his gratitude to our citizens for the great favors shown him. — An excellent idea! — Yes, yes, a child of Dingsda must make our first statue.—

O'KEEFE. (*Bows pleasantly.*)

PLETZER. I shall write to Sevenshoe at once. Ere his arrival, however, I will consult with the town council ; state to them our plans and views, and they will, without doubt, agree with us so that we will be enabled to carry out our intentions without further delay.—I. for my choice, would like the statue to represent a rider sitting on a mule. That would make an immense and novel showing, and cause our Krautwinkel friends to become intensely jealous.

O'KEEFE. Ah, yes, a rider statue! (*Speaks hesitatingly.*) But, pray tell me, Lord Pletzer, whom shall our statue represent?

PLETZER. (*At loss.*)

O'KEEFE. I mean in whose honor shall we erect the statue?

PLETZER. (*Dumfounded; but speaks very de-termined.*) In whose honor the statue shall be erected, you will learn later. Go, and attend to your business, and withhold our plans from the people until I grant you permission to make them public. Do you hear?

O'KEEFE. *Exit.*

PLETZER. (*Sits and meditates.*) How can it be possible—to erect a statue and not know for whom or in whose honor. The thought of erecting a monument so enthused my mind that I never thought for whom the same should be made! This, however, shall not banish my great plans and hopes. No, I will consult the old records of Dingsda where I might be able to find a wise, learned, brave, courageous, pious. and heroic Dingsdaer personage. (*Goes to the library.*) Let me see—my predecessor's name was Huber. I will look for his name (*Opens a large book.*) H, h, h, where is "h" anyway;— ah, here it is! (*Reads.*) Hair, Horn. Horn, Holber, Huber; Ah (*reads:*) Casper Huber, born 29th of February, 1804 at Dingsda; died A. D. 1853. He was a fine shoemaker and a good burgomaster. His wife's name was Anna, Marie, Anastasia Kunigunda Huber, *nee* Fuchtel;

she had six children,—Joseph Huber— — — —.
No, for making shoes we can't erect a statue;
that would be going a little too far. (*Turns the
leaves of the book and reads*)   Maeher, Mayer,
chimney sweeper of Dingsda — (*reads a number
of names in a scarcely audible tone*)   No, this
book does not contain a single prominent
personage. (*Takes another book from the shelf*)
Twelfth Century.   (*Opens book; reads quietly;
turns the pages rapidly, and casts the book aside*)
Pshaw!   during the entire twelfth century
nothing happened save that an old lady poisoned
her husband and was hung for the crime.
(*Looks at other volumes; opens several; reads
softly to himself. Finally, upon opening one book,
a paper clipping falls out : he picks it up and
reads :*)   Ah, what's this!

  Algeria.
        In   the   decisive   battle   fought
between the Stranger-legion and the Arabs,
a battalion of German farmers fought
bravely and heroically.   The bravest of the
brave was a certain Mr. Schmitt.   His
heroism actually won the battle.   The
Stranger-legion was about on the point of
surrendering when the said Schmitt, grasp-
ing the banner from a dead soldier and

waving it over his head, led the Legion against the Arabs a second time. The fight which ensued was a terrific one; but the German soldiers with their new leader soon predominated and routed the entire Arabian army. After the battle the heroic Schmitt could nowhere be found, and it is supposed that he was killed in the thickest of the fight and lies buried beneath the ruins. He deserves to be prominently mentioned with the names of Alexander, Washington, and Constantine.—

(*Pletzer places his hand on his forehead.*)

How did this paper find its way into this volume? What relation has this great deed with — — —

(*Turns the leaves of a volume and finally reads.*)

Frederick Schmitt, born November 23, 1830, at Dingsda; was baptized December 2; attended the public school here, but excelled neither in diligence nor in good conduct. • After the completion of his school term he entered into the services of councilman Pletzer as a waiter at the latter's inn. He was soon after promoted to chief cook, but for some reason or other he was dismissed from service and mysteriously disappeared from Dingsda. It is supposed that he joined the Stranger-legion and went to Africa.—

At last I have him! (*Closes book.*) At last I found a renowned character who is more than worthy to have a monument erected in his honor! — (*Smiling.*) Who would have ever dreamt it; this Schmitt whose sponsor I am; whom I dismissed for putting too much Spanish pepper in the sauce. He, however, persisted that this Spanish pepper was very healthy, but my guests were not of the same opinion, and many of them complained of feeling ill after each meal. I endeavored to persuade Schmitt to stop using the strong spice, but in vain. Finally I was obliged to discharge him. — Well, well, what singular things come to pass! I am really the prime cause of all of Schmitt's great deeds of heroism; for had I not dismissed him from my service, he would not have gone to Africa; and had he not gone to Africa he would not have become a hero, and no monument would be erected in his honor.—If I had known those days how famous a man Frederick Schmitt would some day be, I surely would not have treated him so harshly and forbidden him to play with my son Aloys. Who ever dreamed that Frederick Schmitt would some day become the model for a memorial! I wonder what Mrs. Brummelberger will say when she learns that her nephew will be so highly honored. — I will go immediately to consult the Town Council regarding the matter, and I am satisfied that my plans and views will receive their favorable consideration.

(Puts on his coat. Exit.)

(Calls) O'Keefe, O'Keefe! *(O'Keefe enters)* O'Keefe, follow me to the town hall, where I must consult with the Town Council on the statue matter. Right about, face, march!

END OF ACT I.

ACT II.

....

MARKET PLACE IN DINGSDA.

Pletzer's Inn is on the right side of the street, in front of which are small tables and several chairs.

———

Pletzer is standing in the doorway, wearing a long white apron; several councilmen are grouped around him.

FIRST COUNCILMAN.   Well, Lord Pletzer, when will the statue be placed upon the pedestal?

SECOND COUNCILMAN.   How will the unveiling be celebrated?

THIRD COUNCILMAN.   Have you seen the statue already; is it beautiful?

FOURTH COUNCILMAN. Lord burgomaster, you have a wise head; you will become a famous man; may we ask you for a description of Dingsda's famous work of art?

PLETZER. (*Feels flattered*) Oh, gentlemen, dear gentlemen, do not question too much! Be patient! I have promised the artist Sevenshoe not to reveal anything, and a man in my stand-ing must keep his promise. The time of the unveiling of the statue will be announced to you in due time; therefore be patient! I am the superintendent of the whole undertaking, and believe me, dear gentlemen, the work is in com-petent hands.

FIRST COUNCILMAN. Excuse me, my Lord, for asking: will the Schmitt monument be made after one of his recent portraits?

PLETZER. Patience, patience, my dear sub-jects! Place your confidence in my intelligence. I am doing everything possible to achieve an artistic success for Dingsda, and I will succeed.

FIRST COUNCILMAN. Oh, if only the statue were completed! I am so anxious to see it!

SECOND COUNCILMAN. I hope the weather will be favorable on the unveiling day.

THIRD COUNCILMAN.   Yes, I hope so too. And may the day be very hot, so that the refreshing beer will flow freely.

FOURTH COUNCILMAN.   If only the Krautwinklers will not complete their statue before ours.

FIRST COUNCILMAN.   Bah!   These stupid Krautwinklers with their ignorant Flinzer, the almanac maker!

SECOND COUNCILMAN.   They are foolish for erecting a monument in honor of a crazy book maker.

THIRD COUNCILMAN.   But who dares to call the Dingdaers foolish?   A man like Schmitt really deserves more than a monument.   He was a second Washington, a second Columbus, a second Napoleon!

THIRD COUNCILMAN.   Three cheers for Fritz Schmitt the Great of Dingdsa.   Hurrah!

(*They cheer.   The town clock strikes 9.*)

PLETZER.   (*Rising*)   Fellow citizens!   (*Applause*)   I have the great honor to notify you that in our to-day's session we will discuss mat-

ters pertaining to the celebrated Schmitt statue.
(*Applause*) Just wait a moment till I take off
my apron and put on my burgomaster coat. I'll
return immediately. (*Exit*)

(*Guests rise. The Councilmen form into groups
and discuss matters among themselves. O'Keefe
and Pletzer enter.*)

PLETZER. (*Stamps with his cane.*) Gentlemen, I now call this meeting to order.

FIRST COUNCILMAN. But where shall we sit
down?

ALL. Yes, where shall we sit down?

PLETZER. Silence, you have nothing to say
here! Am I not the burgomaster of Dingsda?

ALL. Yes, yes! Certainly!

PLETZER. Well, then! (*Hawks*) Fellow-
citizens and members of the town council!
Great Applause.

PLETZER (*Loud*) Silence! We live in a
time —

ALL. Very good, very good!

PLETZER. If you interrupt me again, I will
not say another word!

SECOND COUNCILMAN. Well, I'm sure we are allowed to say something too! What are we councilmen for!

PLETZER. You may talk as much as you please when I have finished. But I *must* and *will* have silence when I am speaking. Do you hear?

ALL. Yes, yes! You are right, Mr. Burgomaster! He's allright! (*Applause*)

PLETZER. (*Very angry*) Silence! You get me all confused; what was I going to say yet —

THIRD COUNCILMAN. Pardon me, Mr. Pletzer, but you said something about a speech!

ALL. Yes, a speech, a speech!

O'KEEFE. Please do me the favor and give us a speech. (*Applause*)

PLETZER. Potz Donner! I must have silence! Who is the king of Dingsda, you or I?

ALL. Pletzer is our king. (*Applause*)

PLETZER. Silence! Fellow-citizens, I herewith open the discussion of the unveiling of the Schmitt monument to be erected in Dingsda. Officer O'Keefe will now read to you the letter received from the sculptor Sevenshoe.

O'KEEFE. (*Has his back turned to the audience and reads*) To the wise and esteemed council of Dingsda, Greeting!

Great Applause.

PLETZER. (*Stamping with his cane.*) For the third and last time, *silence!*—Continue, O'Keefe.

O'KEEFE. (*Reads.*) The undersigned hereby notifies a highly esteemed burgomaster and a wise council, that the Schmitt memorial cannot be finished by next Sunday the 13th, but that four more weeks will be required to complete the great masterpiece. The esteemed council will fully comprehend that such a colossal undertaking which shall adorn the city for ever, ought not be over-hastened. I desire to make for Dingsda a statue. that will excel the finest one on the globe, but in order to do this and to evade all future criticism, I am necessitated to ask for a prolonging of one more month.

Respectfully,

Caspar Sevenshoe.

PLETZER. (*After a pause.*) Gentlemen, what remains to be done?

FIRST COUNCILMAN. My opinion is to let the Sevensleeper — —

PLETZER. (*Stamps.*) Sevenshoe!

FIRST COUNCILMAN. Oh, I beg pardon, Mr. Pletzer; I mean Sevenspoon — no Sevencoon — Great Jupiter, what's his name, anyway?

ALL. (*Scream.*) Seven*shoe!*

FIRST COUNCILMAN. O, yes, Sevenshoe, — to come at once; perhaps we can reason with him and induce him to finish the job in two weeks.

PLETZER. (*Angry Speaks to himself.*) Blockhead! That this thought did not enter my mind ere this!

FIRST COUNCILMAN. Blockhead! Do y o u perhaps mean me, Mr. Pletzer? Or do any of the gentlemen present feel guilty? (*All shake their heads.*) What, no one has a word to say?—Very well, then I am the blockhead. — O'Keefe, put the blockhead in your minutes.

O'KEEFE. (*Writes.*)

PLETZER. Silence, silence! I call you to order! I am the presiding officer of this meeting, and everything must go according to my desire. (*All grumble.*) Where is my respect as burgomaster. Am I the blockhead or the burgomaster?

ALL. Pletzer is our burgomaster! He's all right!

PLETZER. (*Shakes hand with First Councilman*) I beg your pardon for calling you a blockhead. But now to business!

ALL. Yes, yes, to business, to business!

PLETZER. The motion of Councilman Berger to request the artist Sevenshoe to come at once to Dingsda is now brought before the meeting. All in favor of this motion will signify it by stepping with me to the right.

(*Pletzer goes to the right. All follow and stamp with their canes.*)

PLETZER. The motion is u n a n i m o u s l y accepted. But not to prove that the motion was fully understood, I request all those who do *not* favor the same to go with me to the left side.

(*All follow Pletzer to the left.*)

PLETZER. Unanimously rejected! Now, gentlemen, this will not do! We must cast a vote per acclamation: Shall the sculptor Sevenshoe be summoned before the council or not?

ALL. Yes, yes; sure, sure; certainly!

PLETZER. O'Keefe, go and seek Sevenshoe, and bring him here. *(O'Keefe exit)* Another question to be discussed is: What festivity shall take place in connection with the unveiling of the Schmitt statue.

FIRST COUNCILMAN. I think we ought to invite all the emperors and kings of the world!

SECOND COUNCILMAN. And have twenty young ladies dressed in white!

THIRD COUNCILMAN. All the school children should sing a national hymn!

FOURTH COUNCILMAN. One million programmes should be printed and scattered all over the world!

FIRST COUNCILMAN. Splendid, splendid! I think our burgomaster ought to write to the President of the United States and ask him to attend!

SECOND COUNCILMAN. And all the houses,

barns, and stables of Dingsda should be decorated with flags and bunting!

THIRD COUNCILMAN.   And Belstead's Military Band ought to be engaged!

FOURTH COUNCILMAN.   Yes; and Mr. Pletzer
ought to deliver an address of welcome!

PLETZER.   (*Holds his hands before his eyes and
stamps with his feet*)   Silence, silence!   For
heaven's sake!   Oh, how my eyes pain me!   I
wish the unveiling day was over already.

(*Enter O'Keefe with Sevenshoe.*)

PLETZER.   Ah, here you are, my dear Sevenshoe!   But now tell me: When will the statue
be completed?

ALL.   Yes, yes.   When will it be unveiled?

SEVENSHOE.   Gentlemen, I am extremely
sorry for being obliged to ask your kind indulg-
ence, for you readily understand that to complete
a work of art requires ample time.   I absolutely
need more time.

PLETZER.   But, my dear Mr. Sevenshoe, will
you not permit me to take at least one glance in
your sanctum?   You have up to date not per-

mitted anyone to see the nearly completed statue; even I myself, the ruler of Dingsda, have been deprived of this singular honor; but my patience is now giving out, and I ask you, dear Mr. Sevenshoe, to permit me to see the wonderful statue, so that I may satisfy these dispairing minds and hearts.

SEVENSHOE. (*Makes a refusing motion with his hand.*)

PLETZER. Then you should bear in mind that you ought to be grateful towards me for entrusting you with a work which is causing your fame, and that I can compel you to show me the progress of your undertaking.

SEVENSHOE. I am indeed very sorry, Lord Burgomaster, for being obliged to disappoint you; and I must refer you to one point of our contract, which reads: "No person shall be permitted to see the statue previous to its unveiling," for this may cause disastrous results and the complete discouragement of the young artist.

PLETZER. Well, if that's the case, I will not molest you; but I want you to promise me faithfully to have the statue completed within a fort-hight, as it is impossible for me to defer the unveiling any longer.

SEVENSHOE. (*Walking up and down in medi= tation*) Well, I'll see what I can do. But you well understand that if I am requested to do a two days' task in one day I must necessarily have more strength; therefore I request you to give me during the coming two weeks daily: Ten extra bottles of beer, four bottles of champagne, a splendid dinner and supper with chicken and oysters, also some fine imported cigars. Do you unanimously agree to do this?

ALL. Yes, yes ; we do!

PLETZER. Well, Mr. Sevenshoe, if this new bill of fare will cause you to complete the statue fourteen days earlier, I will also say *yes !* and you may be my constant guest during the coming two weeks.

SEVENSHOE. Good. The bargain then is struck! Here is my hand. (*Pletzer shakes his hand.*)

ALL. Three cheers for Mr. Sevenshoe!

(*They cheer and then take Sevenshoe upon their shoulders and carry him across the stage. Cur-tain.*)

END OF ACT II.

ACT III.

....

MARKET PLACE IN DINGSDA.

Pletzer's Inn is on the right side of the street, in front of which are small tables and several chairs.

———

The houses are decorated with flags and wreaths. Crowds of people pass to and fro.)

O'KEEFE. (*Enters hastily*) What's the matter here? Leave this place instantly. The assembly of more than one person is not permitted here!

(*People grumble*)

STEIGER (*a citizen*) What are you talking about? The invitation reads that everyone should be present, and that we are allowed to assemble here.

O'KEEFE. That's all right! All may assemble, but everyone for himself, not all together.

(*People laugh and giggle.*)

SCHAFSTALL (*a farmer*) Don't get angry, friend O'Keefe; we are guests of Dingsda today, therefore you ought not to get angry. But stay, O'Keefe, is the statue beautiful?

O'KEEFE. I can't tell—no one has ever seen it. But I am informed that the statue excels any upon the world.

STEIGER. Ah, ha! we are curious to see it! We knew this Schmitt quite well.

(*Sevenshoe approaches in the background. O'Keefe sees him, raises his hat and shouts*)

O'KEEFE. Three cheers for our great Dingsda artist the eminent Sevenshoe — hurrah — again, hurrah — again, hurrah!

(*People join in and swing their hats*)

SEVENSHOE. (*Comes forth very modestly and makes a bow*) I thank you heartily, my dear friends and fellow citizens. (*People shout again*) My dear Mr. O'Keefe, have you seen our Burgomaster Pletzer today?

O'KEEFE. He is still at the town hall, but he instructed me to superintend the transportation of the statue on the pedestal. Can it be removed pretty soon, Mr. Sevenshoe ? The unveiling. as you well know, takes place in two hours.

SEVENSHOE. (*Gives a deep. despairing sigh.*)

STEIGER. Truly, dear sir, it must displease you very much to see so many ignoramuses standing around anxious to see your creation.

ALL. Unveil it, unveil it !

O'KEEFE. Dear Sevenshoe, will no one get to see the statue before its unveiling?

SEVENSHOE. (*Smilingly shakes his head.*) Do not trouble yourself, for all has been attended to.

Exit amid the cheers of the populace.

O'Keefe returns to the town hall. The people disperse after teasing two policemen, who run after some boys, and remain behind the scene. A man in disguise enters. It is Schmitt. He looks about in amazement.

SCHMITT. What's the matter here? Why these decorated houses? These flags and buntings. This private box in the middle of the street? Is to-day the king's birthday? Wait, I will look in my day book.

He takes a book from his pocket, supports his body on a cane and reads. Sevenshoe, not noticing him, passes behind him, strikes against the cane, and causes Sevenshoe to fall to the ground.

SEVENSHOE. Well, well, you crazy fool, this is no dancing platform, this is a public street.

SCHMITT. Oh, beg pardon a thousand times, I did not mean to hurt you; it was quite accidental. But, who is this speaking to me if I may ask?

SEVENSHOE. (*Aside.*) This fellow delights me. I will answer him, he may be of some service to me. (*Loud.*) I am glad to meet you; my name is Sevenshoe and I am here on an artistic tour.

SCHMITT. Ah well, that is delightful! So you are a travelling artist? Then you and I are companions. I have been traveling for the past four weeks without a cent of money; is'nt that an artistic tour?—

SEVENSHOE. (*Aside.*) I am getting to like this fellow more and more. (*Loud.*) You interest me exceedingly, sir. May I ask from whence you came and with what I can serve you?

SCHMITT. O my, that is a long, long story. Here, don't you wish to take a seat? (*Takes off his coat, spreads it upon the floor, sits down upon it, and requests Sevenshoe to sit down also. The latter complies with his wishes.*) Now you see, I come direct from Paprica.

SEVENSHOE. You mean Africa, I presume; but how in the world did you get there?

SCHMITT. That is a still longer story which I shall endeavor to relate now. But do not interrupt me, for if you do, I will not utter another word.

SEVENSHOE. Well, then, go on!

SCHMITT. Once upon a time there was — —

SEVENSHOE. O my! (*gaps*)

SCHMITT. Pst! (*He relates very emphatically*) Once upon a time it happened that I joined the stranger legion and went to Africa. Then I was taken prisoner and made the cook of a sheik. One time it happened that I put too much Spanish pepper in the sauce and this should have caused the death of an Arab. Others learning

this persecuted me and even sought my life. —
I escaped, on my arrival in America— —

PLETZER. (*Without*) O'Keefe, ha, ha, ha —

*Sevenshoe in the meantime went to sleep and
begins to snore. Schmitt notices this and taps him
on the shoulder and tries to wake him, but in vain.
The burgomaster's voice is heard in the back of
the scene.*)

PLETZER. This is the long sought-for day,
O'Keefe; the greatest one Dingsda will ever see.

O'KEEFE. You are quite right, Lord Burgomaster !

SCHMITT. (*To himself*) Why, that is my
friend's voice. I wonder if he still remembers
me. What is he talking about at any rate?

(*Rises, stumbles over Sevenshoe, who on hearing
the noise make a hasty exit. Schmitt, however,
remains on the scene to ascertain what Pletzer and
O'Keefe are talking about.*)

PLETZER. (*Enters with O'Keefe*) Is the
statue on the pedestal already, O'Keefe?

O'KEEFE. (*Very angry*) Well, well; what
does Sevenshoe think of anyway? Such a statue

can not be placed on a pedestal like a candle upon a table !

(*Schmitt approaches the speakers.*)

PLETZER. (*To O'Keefe*) Go to Sevenshoe and bring him here at once. Do you hear ?

O'KEEFE. I go, my lord. (*Gives salute to Pletzer, and in making a military turn he collides with Schmitt, and cries*) Be Gorrah ! Get off the earth, you fool !

SCHMITT. (*Trembling.*)

PLETZER. Make haste, O'Keefe !

O'KEEFE. (*To Schmitt*) How did you get here you good-for-nothing rascal ? You seem to be a hard case ! Did you hear me ?

PLETZER. (*Impatient*) Well, well, O'Keefe, make haste and bring young Sevenshoe before me.

O'KEEFE. (*Staring at Schmitt*) I'll keep an eye on you—take care. Have your papers ready by the time I return !

PLETZER. (*Angry*) Will you get now !

O'KEEFE. I go at once ! (*Looks angrily at Schmitt till he is off the stage.*)

SCHMITT. (*Recovering from his fright approaches and addresses Pletzer*) Excuse me, dear, esteemed sir, you are celebrating a great festival today, I presume?

PLETZER. Well, well; you must indeed have come a great distance if you don't know anything about it.

SCHMITT. Yes—indeed—I—I came from a great distance—and will you be so kind and tell me what celebration takes place here today?

PLETZER. The reigning burgomaster, whom you behold before you (*very dignified*), will today unveil a statue erected in honor of a Dingsda child. The unveiling takes place at 12 o'clock.

SCHMITT. (*Astonished*) A statue! A Dingsda child! And pray tell me, who was this heroic child?

PLETZER. The celebrated Schmitt.

SCHMITT. Schmitt! Schmitt! What Schmitt?

PLETZER. (*Very tragic*) There is but one Schmitt of Dingsda. Who ever would have thought of it, my dear friend! Why, I chased him away for always putting red pepper into the sauce. After leaving Dingsda he joined the Stranger-legion and went to Africa—

SCHMITT. Hm, hm! (*Coughs. Aside*) Great heavens, why I am that Schmitt; how is it possible that they erect a statue in my honor, for I am still among the living.

PLETZER. (*Aside*) My statements must have made a deep impression on the stranger. (*Loud to Schmitt*) And this Schmitt breathed his last on the burning sands of Algeria!

SCHMITT. (*Aside*) Ah, ha! so I am considered dead! But I can't understand why the people want to erect a statue in my honor.

PLETZER. (*Interrupting*) And in remembrance of his great deeds, we will today unveil a rider statue in his honor; but since the horse would have cost too much we concluded to erect only the rider's figure.

SCHMITT. (*Shaking his head doubtfully*) But —if I am permitted to ask—what did this renowned Schmitt do at any rate to receive such distinction?

PLETZER. He performed the noblest deeds of bravery; he excited the greatest admiration throughout Europe ; he fought until the last for the sake of civilization ; he—

SCHMITT. (*Aside*) This is very good. They mean, undoubtedly, my collegian Schmid, from Krautwinkel, whose name ends in d.

PLETZER. What are you saying? Are those not splendid deeds?

SCHMITT. (*Smiling*) Exceedingly splendid! Exceedingly splendid! And how about the statue ; is it already completed?

PLETZER. (*Doubtfully.*(Well, if the same shall be unveiled at 12 o'clock it surely must be completed. But these artists are queer fellows. Just think of it! Our artist, a man by the name of Sevenshoe, also a child of Dingsda, would not allow anyone, for the past ten months, to view his creation ; not even me, the political head of this great city.

(*The town-clock strikes eleven*)

PLETZER. (*Aroused*) Eleven o'clock already! (*Wipes the perspiration from his brow*) Eleven o'clock, and O'Keefe has not yet returned. It seems as though I am betrayed and kept for a fool. Pardon me, my dear sir ; I am obliged to leave you now, for I will be very busy during the next hour. First of all I must find young Sevenshoe, therefore farewell. Or do you desire to accompany me? You may stop at my hotel, "Hotel of the Golden Ox," a first class house with a fine location to view the unveiling; well, shall we go?

SCHMITT. With the greatest of pleasure, Lord Governor.

They cross to the hotel opposite arm in arm. Aloys runs to meet his father.

PLETZER. (*To Aloys*) Aloys, have you seen Mr. Sevenshoe?

ALOYS. No, father, I have not seen him to-day. You know he very seldom comes early, since we tap the first keg of beer at noon.

PLETZER. (*Angry*) What! You have not seen him today yet! And O'Keefe does not return! Well, I guess I'll have to go and look for them. (*Is about to depart when he turns suddenly*) Aloys, I nearly forgot to tell you. This stranger wishes a room toward the front, and a good breakfeast. You may also prepare for him for dinner. (*Whispers to Aloys*) The gentleman comes from a great distance and is traveling incognito. (*To Schmitt*) Farewell, my dear sir?

(*Exit*)

ALOYS. (*Aside*) This is a nice incognito! I will ask him a few questions. (*Loud*) Please take a seat. You come from a great distance, I presume.

SCHMITT. (*Bows assent*)

ALOYS. You just came in due time to take active part in today's great festival. Poor Schmitt!

SCHMITT. You surely feel sad over the fate of Schmitt.

ALOYS. Indeed, I do. We grew up together; that is, he was grown up already when I was born. He liked me very much, and used to tell me beautiful stories and give me fine cakes and eatables—for he was our nurse-girl, cook, chambermaid, hostler, porter, baker, scrub- and washwoman, and everything else. O, how I long to see his face once more.

SCHMITT. (*Touched*) This will please poor Schmitt very much if he hears of it.

ALOYS. How? What do you say? He died a long time ago. Did you know him?

SCHMITT. Why, he was my best friend.

ALOYS. Then you must have been with him in Africa! O, please tell me something about him.

SCHMITT. I will tell you all after breakfast. But permit me to state that he spoke very highly of you and your father. He often told me that he loved you as well as he did his own brother.

ALOYS. (*Takes Schmitt by the hand*) O, then you must be my friend and I will instruct my father to treat you royally. Poor Mrs. Brummelberger! She surely would have died much easier had she only heard one word from her lamented nephew.

SCHMITT. What? Mrs. Brummelberger dead?

ALOYS. Yes, sir! She died, leaving her entire estate to Hans Schmitt. But, alas, the poor fellow departed this life without enjoying these earthly treasures.

SCHMITT. (*Triumphantly*) Hurrah, hurrah! Mrs. Brummelberger is dead! (*Stops suddenly*) Lord have mercy on her poor soul!

ALOYS. (*Astonished.*) Well, well, why are you jubilant? What interests you so much sir?

Is it perhaps the death of Mrs. Brummelberger?
You are not — —

SCHMITT. (*Takes Aloys' hand*) Why certainly
I am. Who else. Don't you know — (*At this
juncture Pletzer calls in back of scene: O'Keefe!
O'Keefe!*)

SCHMITT. (*Lets go of Aloys' hand and runs
towards the house.*) Will you please serve my
breakfast now?

ALOYS. (*Aside*) I cannot understand this
person. (*Bewildered.*)

Exit.

PLETZER. (*Enters, holding O'Keefe by the coat
collar*) Where have you been loafing about? I
have been searching for you for the past hour!
Where is young Sevenshoe? Did you find him?
Speak, or I will break your right leg!

O'KEEFE. I could not find Sevenshoe any-
where. The whole affair looks very suspicious
to me.

PLETZER. (*Lets go of O'Keefe*) What do you
mean to say? Express yourself more clearly.
Speak!

O'KEEFE. Listen! As I passed the town-hall in search of Sevenshoe, I met a soldier who was sent by the king. "O'Keefe," said he, in a very excited tone of voice, "a suspicious looking individual is loafing about this town. I am sent by the Royal chief of police to notify all guardians of the peace to be on the alert and arrest all suspicious looking characters on sight." Then he spurred his horse and hastily departed.

PLETZER. Well, what has this to do with young Sevenshoe?

O'KEEFE. Nothing at all. I don't refer to him!

PLETZER. Well, whom do you refer to then, you blockhead!

O'KEEFE. Thanks for the compliment. I refer to the person with the long beard.

(*Aloys appears at the door*)

PLETZER. (*To Aloys*) Where is the stranger, Aloys?

ALOYS. He is eating his breakfast, father!

O'KEEFE. (*Runs toward the door*) Ah, ha, I'll make him show his papers.

PLETZER. (*Holds O'Keefe by the coat tail*) O'Keefe, don't arrest him until he has paid for his breakfast! Do you understand?

O'KEEFE. Allright, Lord Pletzer. But I will go in and watch him closely. (*Exit in house*)

PLETZER. I am almost frantic! Young Sevenshoe has been seen nowhere! What remains to be done? The only course left open for me is to force the door leading to his studio.

ALOYS. But, father, you know that he has expressly forbidden for any one to enter his studio, therefore you better wait a few moments; perhaps he will come.

(*Sevenshoe enters thoughtlessly but recedes upon beholding Pletzer*)

PLETZER. No, no, I can't wait any longer. In half an hour the unveiling shall take place, and it would be a great wrong to disappoint the assembled people. Adieu, Aloys! I will cause the door to be burst open and order the statue to be placed upon the pedestal. (*Exit*)

(*Sevenshoe again enters, makes a nose at Pletzer, and walks towards Aloys*)

ALOYS. My God, Mr. Sevenshoe, where have you been all morning. My father has been looking for you; he just left this moment; hasten, and you will yet catch him.

SEVENSHOE. O dear youg Pletzer, I can't run after your father, for a great secret burdens my heart; will you not aid me?

ALOYS. A secret? I shall aid you? Why, man you are talking nonsence or else jesting.

SEVENSHOE. No, no, dear Aloys, I am not talking nonsense nor am I jesting. Oh I am in a terrible predicament—I owe your father *so* much.

ALOYS. Be calm, my dear sir; you owe my father nothing! He, in fact, owes you a great deal for making the statue.

SEVENSHOE. O Aloys, have mercy on one who is given to despair.

ALOYS. (*Aside*) Well, now, this is a nice how-d'-do! I wonder what ails him anyway. (*Loud*) Mr. Sevenshoe, please tell me what is marring your happiness on this great festive day? Have you perhaps received bad news?

SEVENSHOE. Bear with me, dear Aloys, whilst I speak, and do not judge me too severely.

You will remember that when I attended school at the old log cabin, back of your father's farm, I was so fascinated with drawing that my teacher told me that I had great genius and ought to devote all my spare time in cultivating this art. I did so, and my drawings were eagerly sought by all the pupils at the old school.

ALOYS   Yes, I know that, Mr. Sevenshoe; for do you remember the picture you drew representing Moses in the bullrushes?

SEVENSHOE.   Yes, quite well

ALOYS.   Well, that picture is now in my possession, and adorns the wall of my bedroom. But, Mr. Sevenshoe, what have these drawings to do with your sadness?

SEVENSHOE.   Very much. dear Aloys.   For when I left school I was engaged by Mr. Dauber, the painter, and worked at his studio as an apprentice for some time, but received no pay. This caused me to give up my position—and then my misfortune began.   Oh, do not judge me too severely after you have heard my tale—

ALOYS.   Go on, Mr. Sevenshoe.

SEVENSHOE.   Well, Aloys, I will tell you all.

—You know that some time ago I was sent to Munich, at the city's expence, to learn the art of sculptoring — —

ALOYS.   Well, well, and — —

SEVENSHOE.   Well, I can't say that I *lost* all my time, but instead of learning the art of sculpturing I spent most of my time in playing billiards and poker.

ALOYS.   Then you did not learn the sculptor's art ?

SEVENSHOE.   (*Sadly*) No, I know nothing of it.

ALOYS.   And how about the statue?

SEVENSHOE.   Alas! I have none to show.

ALOYS.   Why, Sevenshoe. you are a fraud !

SEVENSHOE.   Well, just as you say.

ALOYS.   I never thought that you were so impertinent.   By your actions you have not only deceived my father but the entire city of Dingsda.

SEVENSHOE.   Pardon me, Aloys, but I must say that I did not deceive the city ; I only promised in my contract to *furnish* a statue, not to *make* one and was always in hopes that some day one might be found, but, alas, none has yet turned up.

ALOYS. (*Meditating*) But, pray tell me, how can I be of assistance to you?

SEVENSHOE. Very easily. You knew Schmitt, my supposed model quite well, in fact, you resemble him greatly. Perhaps you can find some of his old clothes and put them on ——

(*A cry of* "Help, Help" *is heard from the hotel. Aloys and Sevenshoe listen; Doors are heard slammed; chairs and tables are upset, dishes and glasses broken; foot steps are heard.*)

SEVENSHOE. (*Bewildered*) Please, Aloys, consider the matter and save me! I will bear all responsibilities. (*Exit to back of scene*)

SCHMITT. (*Enters upon the scene screaming. He has been ordered out of the hotel by O'Keefe.*) Save me, dear Aloys, save me!

SEVENSHOE. (*Peeps from behind the scene and sees Schmitt.*)

ALOYS. (*To Schmitt*) Have you finished your breakfast already?

SCHMITT. (*Excited*) No, no, that's just what worries me the most. As I was enjoying my breakfast, the police sergeant came in, took a seat opposite mine, and watched me intently. All of a sudden he sprang to his feet like a maniac; caught me by the coat-collar and began abusing me. I jumped up and hit him in the face with my egg-cup which stunned him. This gave me an opportunity of running out of doors. But this wild man may appear at any moment and arrest me; therefore save me, dear friend save me!

ALOYS. But, sir, are you a criminal?

SCHMITT. (*Takes off his false beard*) No, no, I am Schmitt!

ALOYS. What! Is it possible? You are —

SCHMITT. Hans Schmitt of Dingsda, and come direct from Africa.

ALOYS. Great heavens! But, pray tell me, why are you a criminal?

SCHMITT. In a very innocent way. Soon after joining the Stranger·Legion in Africa, I was taken prisoner and then made cook of a sheik. One time it happened that I put too much

Spanish pepper in the sauce and this should have caused the death of an Arab. Others, learning this, persecuted me and even sought my life. I escaped. On my arrival in America I learned that word had been received from Arabian head-quarters to arrest me. Police officer O'Keefe tried to do so; he is still in the hotel, but may appear on the scene at any moment, and then "farewell" dear Hans.

While Aloys extends to him his hand Sevenshoe rushes forward and pulls Schmitt away.

ALOYS. (*Excited*) What are you doing, Mr. Sevenshoe; surely you do not intend to betray this unhappy man?

SEVENSHOE. No, indeed; just the contrary.

SCHMITT. (*Astonished*) You are very kind, dear sir, but – I – I – do not quite understand— –

SEVENSHOE. Follow me, and I will lead you to a place where neither police nor detectives will ever discover you. Come, come, make haste.

(He takes Schmitt by the hand. The latter follows reluctantly)

ALOYS (*Alone*) Well, well, this proceeding really dumbfounds me. I wonder what he intends to do with poor Hans! I almost believe that Mr. Sevenshoe has lost his reason! Perhaps he intends to betray Schmitt and thereby save himself.

Paces up and down shaking his head doubtfully. Pletzer enters. out of breath and bewildered.

ALOYS. My God, father, what has happened?

PLETZER. Get away from me. Aloys; I've got the hydrophobia! Oh, that confounded, good-for nothing Sevenshoe! If only the rats would eat him!

ALOYS. (*Pretending*) Why, father, what has happened?

PLETZER. I just came from Sevenshoe's workshop. I had the door broken open! And found no sculptor and no statue!

ALOYS. (*Pretending*) And nothing else?

PLETZER. (*Angry*) And nothing else? Is that not enough? What shall I tell the people? In twenty minutes the unveiling is supposed to

take place! Oh, donner und blitzen; what shall
I do; what shall I do!

Paces up and down pulling his hair. O'Keefe
rushes madly out of the hotel.

PLETZER. O'Keefe, where is young Sevenshoe? Have you seen the swindler?

O'KEEFE. What does young Sevenshoe con-
cern me? I am looking for the other fellow—
the fellow with the beard! I can assure you,
Lord Pletzer, he is a criminal of the worst type.
I will have no rest until I bring him behind the
bars.

PLETZER. What do I care for the man with
the beard? Bring me the sculptor; bring forth
the statue, and I will reward you richly.

O'KEEFE. (*Still speaking of Schmitt*) I
noticed the first time I saw him that he was an
escaped criminal, but, just as I say, I'll find him,
and then look out, look out!

Aloys exit. Pletzer and O'Keefe are very
excited; they pace up and down. Seven-
shoe enters unconcernedly and crosses
the stage. Pletzer is dumb-
founded; finally he pushes
O'Keefe against Sev-
enshoe

PLETZER. In the name of the law, arrest that man !

SEVENSHOE. (*Smiling*) You desire to arrest me, Lord Pletzer ! What for, my dear sir?

PLETZER. (*Taking out his watch and holding it under Sevenshoe's nose*) Tremble, wretch ; tremble ! Only ten minutes of twelve ! I come from your workshop !

SEVENSHOE. (*Smiling*) And, pray tell me, what did this visit reveal ?

PLETZER. I looked for the Schmitt statue !

SEVENSHOE. Why, I am really sorry that you have troubled yourself in vain. My statue went out for a walk ; it went out to get good and dry.

PLETZER. (*Very excited*) Sir, do you think you can keep me for a fool?

SEVENSHOE. I don't intend to do anything of the kind. (*Pretends to be sad*) No, no; I never thought that I would receive such treatment on the very day on which I am to present my native city a work of art of my own creation.

PLETZER. (*Astonished*) Speak ; what do you mean ? I don't quite understand.

SEVENSHOE. You know, without doubt, something about "synkocrasy"?

PLETZER. (*Look very wise*) Why, certainly. (*Hawks*) But I would be pleased to hear your opinion of it.

SEVENSHOE. (*Very dignified*) Synkocrasy is that process which gives marble such a natural aspect and color that nature itself could not make it appear more human.

PLETZER. *Meditates for a brief time; then speaks excitedly*) Nonsense, nonsense ; you are only keeping me for a fool. I ask you now for the last time : Where is the statue ?

SEVENSHOE. (*Seemingly insulted*) Why, it is where it belongs.

PLETZER. On its pedestal ?

SEVENSHOE. Why, most assuredly ; where else could it be ?

PLETZER. Then prove it to me this very instant ! Come with me and show me the statue ? I will not believe you until I have seen it.

SEVENSHOE. I will show it to you with the greatest of pleasure. Why, I have been looking for you everywhere in order to get your opinion of the statue ere its unveiling. Come, follow me!

(*Exit arm in arm.*)

END OF ACT III.

ACT IV.

Open place in Dingsda. Street background. In the center is a pedestal enclosed by curtains. On this pedestal stands Schmitt, without beard, and his face well powdered. He is attired in a white costume, holding in his right hand a large spoon. Sevenshoe is leaning against the pedestal and is smiling. Pletzer holds the curtain of tent apart so that the audience gets a view of the interior. Pletzer and O'Keefe gaze upon the statue in amazement.

PLETZER. Donner und blitzen, what a fine likeness of our hero Schmitt!

SEVENSHOE. (*Makes a complimentary bow*).

PLETZER. Especially the right leg and arm. His face is also very good.

SEVENSHOE. (*Smiles and holds his handkerchief before his face.*)

O'KEEFE. (*Looks wildly at the statue.*)

PLETZER. But what a peculiar costume you gave him! I'm sure you don't call that dress a soldier's uniform?

SEVENSHOE. Most assuredly! That is the uniform of the soldiers of the Stranger Legion—all white on account of the severe heat in Africa.

PLETZER. Remarkable! Why, the costume looks for all the word like the dress of a servant—white coat, white pants, white apron, white cap. And what a peculiar weapon he holds in his hand! Why, it looks more like a frying-pan than like a yatagan.

SEVENSHOE. Indeed it does, for the African weapons have a very striking resemblance to our kitchen utensils. But, My Lord, I would be pleased to ascertain whether you are satisfied with my efforts.

PLETZER. I am perfectly pleased with the statue, and herewith congratulate you. (*Shakes his hand*) At the dinner to be given at the town hall I will express my feeling in more appropriate words. I must now hasten to put on another coat and tie before the unveiling begins. Good bye! Come along, O'Keefe.

O'KEEFE. (*Stares at the statue*).

PLETZER. Don't you hear me, O'Keefe; you should follow me. (*Angry*.)

O'KEEFE. (*Gives the statue an enraged glance, then follows Pletzer hesitatingly.*)

SCHMITT. (*After Pletzer and O'Keefe are off*) O, God be praised that they are gone! I could not have stood still much longer. That confounded O'Keefe made me nervous.

SEVENSHOE. Well, make yourself comfortable now, my dear Schmitt, and gain new strength and courage for the unveiling, so that you will not make a botch of the whole affair.

SCHMITT. I'll promise that I'll do my very best, and if the affair does not last too long my services will be gratis.

SEVENSHOE. Adieu, noble "work of art." We shall soon meet again. Farewell until the unveiling. (*Closes the curtain and advances toward the hotel, but is intercepted by Aloys*).

ALOYS. Ah, did I find you at last; tell me immediately: What did you do with Schmitt?

SEVENSHOE. (*Smiling*) I petrified him; that is, turned him into marble.

ALOYS. Leave your jokes aside, Sevenshoe. I must know where my friend Schmitt is at once, or else I will reveal all I know!

SEVENSHOE. (*After some hesitancy*) Well, if you insist upon seeing him then follow me.

Takes Aloys behind the curtain. Schmitt is standing motionless on the pedestal as both enter.

ALOYS. (*Shrieks, then calls to Schmitt*) Well, well, so he has hidden you here!

SCHMITT. And is not the attitude I am requested to assume a peculiar one?

ALOYS. Well, I should say so. I am positive the people will detect this is not a monument.

SEVENSHOE. Oh, no, my dear Aloys; my statue has already stood a severe test; your father nearly went into ecstacy on beholding my wonderful statue.

ALOYS. (*Shakes his head doubtfully.*)

SEVENSHOE. (*With kindness to Aloys*) "The moment decides over the life of man and over his aptness," says Goethe. Reflect upon the truth of this inspired enunciation, and make it the rule of all your undertakings. Dear Aloys, my fate rests in your hands. Solicit for me the pardon of your father for my fraudulent trick, and you shall have the $2,000 reward which the state offers to the person who will cause the apprehension and arrest of this criminal and murderer. (*Points to Schmitt.*)

SCHMITT. (*From pedestal*) Don't do it, dearest Aloys; don't do it!

SEVENSHOE. Do not listen to the pleadings of this lifeless statue; it is a mere humbug.

SCHMITT. Don't let me hear any more of your insulting remarks, Mr. Sevenshore, or else this lifeless statue will give you a sample of its strength. (*Makes fists.*)

SEVENSHOE. You have nothing to say, you good-for nothing rascal; you murderer; you—

SCHMITT. (*Very angry*) Now, that's just enough!

*(Smith throws the spoon or pan aside ;
jumps from the pedestal and fights
with Sevenshoe. Aloys tries to
part them. Schmitt gives
a sudden scream and
runs in the back-
ground.*

ALOYS AND SEVENSHOE. What's the matter?

SCHMITT. (*Hold his nose*) Oh, I got a severe blow on my nose! See how it is bleeding! (*Weeps*).

SEVENSHOE. (*Excited*) Oh, this is fateful! I have destroyed my own work of art.

(*Voices are heard without*).

ALOYS. List! That is my father's voice! I must hide myself. Help yourself as well as you can. (*Exit in back of scene*).

(*Pletzer enters. Sevenshoe stands at the
entrance of the tent holding the curtain so that Pletzer cannot see
the supposed statue*).

PLETZER. In a few moments the unveiling will begin. Mr. Sevenshoe you will stand be-side the statue, so that the people may also be-

hold the artist. Now I will deliver my address.
When I say in fiery tones : "Behold our hero
Schmitt," you will let the curtain drop, and the
people will shout and hail.

SEVENSHOE. Very well, my lord, all is ready.
You may begin your address.

> (*The town clock chimes 12. Part of Or-
> chestra comes on stage and plays.
> People come from all sides.
> O'Keefe and other officers
> are busy keeping back
> the crowd*).

PLETZER. (*Standing on a box, searches all his
pockets*) My goodness, I've lost my address.
O'Keefe, O'Keefe you speak ; I am all confused.

O'KEEFE. Three cheers for Lord Pletzer, our
burgomaster. Hurrah ! Hurrah !! Hurrah !!!
(*All cheer. Musicians cheer ; no music*).

> (*The statue is unveiled. Schmitt again
> poses on the pedestal, but his back
> turned toward the audience. Cheer-
> ing is heard from all sides. Plet-
> zer and O'Keefe are confound
> ed and are staring at Schmitt
> who holds his handker-
> chief before his nose.*

PLETZER. (*After some deliberation*) Why, how is this, Mr. Sevenshoe? Before, as you showed us the statue, its face looked toward the east, and now it is looking west. ´

SEVENSHOE. (*Smiling*) Why, Lord Pletzer, that is a secret joke of mine. I have, namely, arranged a turn table on the pedestal so that the statue can be turned at pleasure.

PLETZER. Ha, ha, ha! That's very practical indeed. But what caused you to turn its back toward the audience at its first unveiling?

SEVENSHOE. Because I wish to surprise them all the more afterward.

PLETZER. (*Impatient*) Well, you better turn the statue now, I think it is the highest time.

SEVENSHOE. (*Embarrassed*) The cheering of the back view has not yet subsided, Lord Pletzer, so we had better wait until we have gained the entire success of the one side ere we expose the other; are you not of the same opinion my dear sire?

PLETZER. Very well, just as you think best. But I for myself want to gaze once more upon the interesting face of my idol.

(*He walks around the statue, but Schmitt
turns just as Pletzer walks, so that
his back is always turned to
ward the latter*).

PLETZER   Ah, ha; now he is turning. That's
wonderful!   That's wonderful!

(*When Schmitt [the statue] faces the
populace they scream, laugh and cheer.
At this instance Sevenshoe trips
Pletzer, who falls to the floor.
The artist? then quickly closes
the curtain.   The people
scream at the top of their
voices, and want to take
the statue by storm;
suddenly a courier
enters with a
telegram.*

COURIER.   Where is Burgomaster Pletzer?
I have an important telegram for him.

(*Pletzer steps forward, takes the message
and reads it in a subdued tone*).

PEOPLE.   (*Crowd around Pletzer and shout*)
Read aloud!   Read!   Read!

*(In the meantime Sevenshoe is trying to
make his escape, but is detained by
some bystanders. After Pletzer
has read a few lines he
drops the message and
stares upon the
floor.*

ALOYS. What's the matter father? Are
you ill?

PLETZER. O misery, misery! Our rejoicing
turns into deep sorrow!

PEOPLE. How so? What's the matter? Is
some one dead? Perhaps the Prince of Wales?

PLETZER. (*Angry*) No, no; nobody is dead!
That's the trouble—he lives, he lives!

PEOPLE. Who lives, who, who! The Prince
of Wales?

PLETZER. No, no; the good for-nothing
Schmitt!

O'KEEFE. Why, that must be a mistake! It
can't be possible!

PEOPLE. Read, read!

PLETZER. (*Reads*) From the Chief of Police:

"It has been discovered that the vagabond
of whom I have already notified the guardians of the peace is a certain Frederick
Schmitt of Dingsda. He has been seen by
some persons strolling through the streets
of your city with a false beard as a disguise,
for he has been accused of poisoning a man,
and on that account his arrest is demanded."

O'KEEFE. (*Joyfully*) I have it! I have it!

(*Forces his way into the tent*).

PLETZER. He is not dead—and I had a statue
erected in his honor! Oh, that is awful; that is
terrible! But I must have my revenge, my
revenge!

(*He grasps the cane of one of the bystanders;
gives the tent a push—it falls. Schmitt,
however, had previously escaped in the
background. Pletzer is dumbfounded,
and stands in a motionless attitude
with his cane uplifted. The people are amazed and shout. Noise
is heard in the background.
O'Keefe enters having
Schmitt by the coat col-
lar. They go to the
foreground.*)

PEOPLE. There's the statue! There's the statue!

O'KEEFE. Yes; a nice statue! It is Schmitt of Dingsda; the same rascal who used to be cook at Lord Pletzer's hotel.

PLETZER. (*Angry*) Wretch, why did you not die in Africa! Now you will end your miserable existence on the gallows. Here, read this.

(*Gives Schmitt the telegram.*)

SCHMITT. (*Trembling, and acts very much frightened. He reads the message to himself, then brightens up and looks courageous*).

PEOPLE. What's the matter? What's the matter?

PLETZER. (*Takes the letter out of Schmitt's hands*) Let me see, I forgot to read the closing lines.

(*Reads*).

' When the said Schmitt is discovered, he should be informed that he has nothing more to fear. The analysis of the sauce which should have caused the death of the Arabian

Abdul Kaban showed that it only contained a strong dose of Spanish pepper. and not poison, as was at first suspected."

PEOPLE. (*Laugh and shout*).

PLETZER. (*To Sevenshoe*) Sir, you shall suffer for all this! You shall be punished to the full extent of the law!

SEVENSHOE. (*Jumps upon the empty pedestal and says*) Sch—sch. *Deep silence follows*).

(*He addresses the multitude*).

"Highly esteemed citizens! You will surely pardon the joke which our worthy and renowned Burgomaster Pletzer has this day played on you especially because the joke was such a great success in all its details. I desire to remind you that today is Mardi Grass, a day on which a joke cannot be taken amiss by such an intelligent class of people as I have the honor to address. You all know that our esteemed burgomaster is noted for his highly amusing tricks, and now, since the capital joke is over, I invite you one and all to dine and drink at your heart's desire at the hotel of The Golden Ox. at our burgomaster's expense.

and after feasting to enjoy dancing until late in the morning. High live our grand, eminent, illustrious, esteemed, intelligent, and renowned Burgomaster Pletzer."

PEOPLE. Hurrah! Hurrah! Hurrah!

PLETZER. (*Aside to Sevenshoe*) You are a rascal, but I thank you for your grand arrangements. (*To the people*) Dear citizens, Mr. Sevenshoe has spoken the truth, the whole truth and nothing but the truth. Hoping that the joke will not displease you, I invite you to my hotel across the way, where we shall drink and feast on the welfare of our living statue.

(*All cheer and leave the stage in procession*).

FINIS.